PAUL MASON

SKATE MONKEY

KIDNAP

ILLUSTRATED BY
ROBIN BOYDEN

BLOOMSBURY EDUCATION
AN IMPRINT OF BLOOMSBURY

LONDON OXFORD NEW YORK NEW DELHI SYDNEY

SKATE MONKEY

Monkey and his friends, Zu and Sandy, lived in the Jade Emperor's Cloud Palace. But they played all sorts of tricks on people, so, as a punishment, the Jade Emperor sent them down to Earth.

They can only return to the Cloud Palace if they prove that they can use their magical powers for good...

CONTENTS

Story inspired by *Monkey* by
Wu Ch' Êng-Ên, c1500–1582

Chapter One

Eva was in the car with her mum. They were on their way home from school. Eva's mum was Sophie B, a famous film star.

As they drove along past the skate park, Eva told her mum a funny story about something that happened in school. They both laughed.

Then, suddenly, a large, dark car drove right across the road in front of them. Mum slammed on the brakes. Their car swerved off the road and skidded to a stop.

Four men jumped out of the dark car. They were dressed in black suits. They wore dark glasses.

"Get down!" Mum shouted to Eva. She locked the doors.

The men walked over to the car. "Grab the girl," the leader shouted. One of the men smashed the car window with a hammer. He reached in and unlocked the doors. Then he opened the door and grabbed Eva. She screamed.

"Stop," cried Eva's mum, trying to hold on to her daughter's jacket.

"Give us two million pounds and you get her back," said the leader with a mean smile. His teeth were like snake fangs. "Don't tell the cops, or you won't see her again."

The men dragged Eva to their car. They shoved her in and drove away.

The dark car sped past the skate park. There were some kids skating. Eva banged on the car window and shouted to them for help.

Chapter Two

In the skate park, Monkey, Zu and Sandy were doing tricks on their skateboards. The skate park was empty. Everyone else had gone home.

The friends heard the screech of car tyres. They saw the dark car speeding down the street. They heard Eva's shouts. They saw her banging on the window.

"Wow! Did you see that?" asked Zu.

"That girl is in trouble!" said Sandy.

"Let's go!" said Monkey.

The three friends ran through the gate, carrying their skateboards. Monkey blew out a long breath of air. He said some magic words. The skateboards began to glow.

Monkey, Zu and Sandy put their boards onto the pavement, and jumped on. The skateboards lifted off from the ground and climbed into the air.

"Come on!" shouted Monkey. He could see the dark car ahead in the distance. It was heading out of town.

The skateboards shot down the road. They began to pick up speed. They started to catch up.

Chapter Three

Monkey, Zu and Sandy zoomed along the country road chasing the car. They could see the men inside. They looked mean.

Eva saw Monkey out of the back window. "Help!" she called out.

It was time to do something. Monkey reached into his jacket. He pulled out his pen. "Full charge," he said. The pen flashed and crackled as it changed shape. The pen grew and grew. Soon it was the size of a baseball bat. Monkey spun it around in his hand.

Sandy got out her smartphone. "Upgrade," she cried. The smartphone changed shape. It became a huge metal pole. Sandy twirled her pole above her head like a helicopter.

Zu reached into his jeans. He pulled out a fork. "Supersize!" He called. The fork glowed like fire. It became bigger and bigger. It turned into a huge metal rake.

"Now!" shouted Monkey. He swerved his skateboard and somersaulted on to the roof of the car. He raised his bat. He brought it down hard. The windscreen cracked into pieces. The driver slammed on the brakes. The car skidded into a ditch. Monkey somersaulted on to the ground. He landed smoothly. Sandy and Zu slid to a stop.

The car doors opened. The four men jumped out. Monkey, Sandy and Zu stood on the side of the road, waiting for them.

"Teach them a lesson!" shouted the leader.

The men charged.

Sandy did a flying kick. One of the men fell to the ground. She twirled her pole, hitting another man. Zu used his rake to squash one man against the car. Monkey somersaulted into the air. He kicked out, knocking the leader down.

Monkey ran to the car. He quickly reached in and held out his hand to Eva. She had tears running down her face. "We are here to save you," he said. "Hop on my back!"

Eva jumped out of the car. She climbed on Monkey's back. She grabbed hold of his shoulders.

"Let's get out of here before they get up," said Monkey.

Chapter Four

The skateboards zoomed down the road. Zu and Sandy rode in front. Monkey followed close behind. Eva clung onto Monkey's back. Monkey spun his skateboard around mid-air to take a look behind.

He could see the dark car. It was back on the road. It was chasing them.

"We need to hide," Monkey called out to Zu and Sandy. Then he saw a sign on the side of the road. It said, "Zoo 1 mile."

"Follow me," said Monkey. He swerved around the corner.

The friends screeched to a stop outside the zoo. The zoo was closed for the night. Monkey shook the gates. From inside the zoo came the sound of monkeys howling.

"They won't think of looking for us here," said Sandy.

"Exactly," said Monkey. He bent down in front of the gate.

He whispered a magic lock-opening spell. The lock clicked open.

Monkey opened the gate. "This way," he said. He shut the gate behind them.

Monkey ran towards the monkey cage. Inside, some black and white monkeys hung from the branches of the trees. They jumped up and down when they saw Monkey. They leapt from tree to tree.

"Great, just what we need: more monkeys," groaned Zu.

Monkey used his lock-opening spell to open the gate to the cage. "In you go, little girl," he said.

"Inside?" said Eva. She looked at the black and white monkeys. She wasn't so sure it was a good idea.

"Don't worry, I am their king," said Monkey.
One of the monkeys held out its tiny hand
to Eva. Eva took its hand and climbed into the
cage.

Zu, Monkey and Sandy followed. They all hid in the bushes. Monkey spoke to the monkeys. The monkeys ran away. They came back with some hay. They made a warm bed for Eva. She sat down.

"We are safe here for the moment," said Monkey.

Chapter Five

Sandy sat down next to Eva. She put her arm around Eva's shoulder. "Now, tell us who you are," said Sandy.

"My name is Eva Baker," said Eva. "My mum is Sophie B."

"The famous movie star?" asked Zu. Eva nodded.

"So that's why those men were trying to kidnap you," said Monkey.

"They told my mum they wanted money," said Eva.

"Well, first let's get you back to your mum. Then we will call the police," said Monkey. "Pass me your phone, Sandy."

Eva told Monkey the number and he dialled it.

"Is that Sophie B? My name is Monkey," he said. "I know this sounds crazy, but we have rescued your daughter. Meet us at the zoo."

Eva's mum cried, "Thank you! Oh, thank you! I'll be right there."

Monkey spoke to the monkeys again. The monkeys ran off. They came back with some

fresh fruit. One of them handed Eva
an apple.

"About time too," said Zu. "I'm starving."

After they had eaten, Monkey waited by the front gate of the zoo. He looked in the dark for Eva's mum. At last, he saw her running across the car park.

Monkey ran up to her. "I'm Monkey," he said. "Eva is safe. She is close by." Monkey opened the zoo gate.

"Just what is going on?" said Eva's mum. "How did you save her?"

"It's a long story," said Monkey. He led Eva's mum into the zoo. "When this is all over, can I get a selfie?" he said with a smile.

At the monkey cage, Monkey gave a whistle.
"It's OK to come out," he called, opening the door.
Eva crawled out from behind the bushes.
"Mum!" she shouted as she ran to her.

"You're safe now," cried Eva's mum,
squeezing her tight.

"Monkey, Zu and Sandy saved me," said Eva.
"They are heroes."

"More like superheroes," said Eva's mum.

From the shadows came a laugh.

"Superheroes? What a joke."

A gang of men stepped out of the darkness. The leader stood at the front. They blocked the path.

"Hello again," said the leader. "Remember me?"

Chapter Six

Monkey did a quick count. There were about ten men in the shadows. All of them mean. All of them looking for a fight.

"Not you again," growled Zu.

"How did you find us?" said Sandy.

The leader held up a tracker. "We put a bug in the girl's jacket. We followed you on GPS. We were waiting to trap you," he said. He turned to Eva's mum. "Have you got the two million pounds?" he asked.

Eva's mum shook her head. "I need more time."

"Then I guess we are taking the girl back," said the leader.

"But you tried that before," said Monkey, "and we beat you."

"Yes, but this time, I'm the one with the tricks," said the leader.

The leader lifted up his arms. Light shot out from his body in all directions like rays from the sun. There was a horrible groaning sound. Then, suddenly, he turned into a huge snake. The snake's scales glowed red hot and its eyes flickered. It had giant fangs, like two swords. "Surprise, surprise," it hissed.

Eva screamed. Her mum pulled her close.

"A snake demon!" gasped Zu.

"Where did that come from?" asked Sandy.

"Full charge!" said Monkey.

"Upgrade!" said Sandy.

"Supersize!" yelled Zu.

The snake laughed. "You take care of the others," it said to its men. "The one with the monkey face is mine."

It turned to Monkey. "Bye, bye," it hissed.

Chapter Seven

The snake demon rushed forward. Its fangs cut through the air. Monkey dodged and rolled to the side. He leapt up high. He brought his bat down as hard as he could.

But the snake moved quickly and knocked Monkey over. It pressed him into the wall. Monkey fell to the ground. His weapon flew from his hand.

The snake slid across the ground. It wrapped itself around Monkey. It squeezed as tightly as it could.

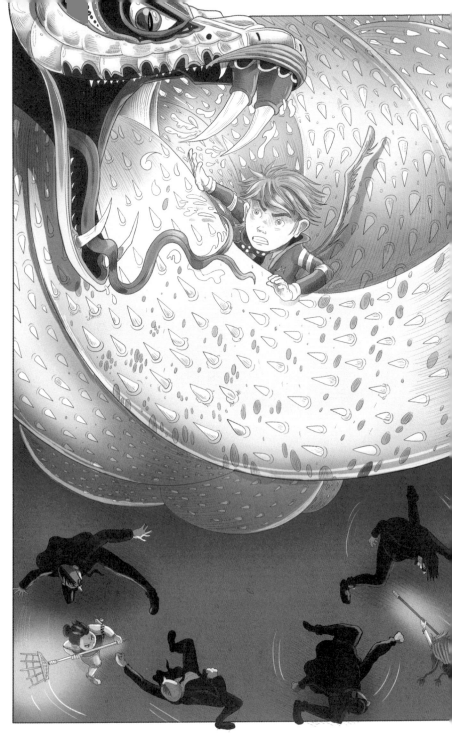

"You should have given up when you had the chance," said the snake.

"Your breath smells!" Monkey cried. He could feel his ribs cracking.

Then, a rock flew out of the darkness. It hit the snake on the head. It was followed by another rock, and then another. The snake hissed, trying to dodge the rocks. "Who dares strike the snake demon?" it hissed.

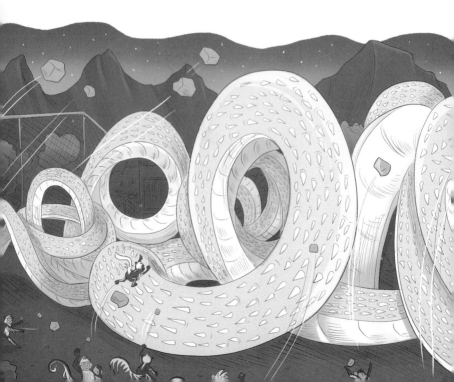

The monkeys screeched. They leapt up and down and threw rock after rock at the snake's head. The snake gave a loud groan and let go of Monkey.

Monkey quickly jumped to his feet. "Eat this," he yelled and he struck the snake demon with his bat. The snake demon fell to the ground.

"Come on, monkeys!" shouted Monkey, and the monkeys charged.

Chapter Eight

The monkeys ran over to the snake demon.
They grabbed its tail. They held it down.
Monkey saw his chance. He held his bat high
in the air over the snake demon. The snake
could not move.

"Game over," said Monkey.

The snake gave a great moan but it lay still. It was frightened of Monkey and his monkey army.

Monkey looked to see how his friends were doing. Zu was standing over a pile of men, swinging his rake. Sandy spun her pole. They could hear the sound of police sirens getting closer.

The snake turned to Monkey. "You win this time," it hissed. "But we will meet again!" There

was a flash of light and a cloud of smoke. Suddenly, the snake vanished into the air.

Eva and her mum crept out of the bushes. "Did that really just happen?" asked Eva's mum.

"Now how about that selfie?" laughed Monkey.

* * *

Monkey, Zu and Sandy were back at the skate park.

Sandy stopped skating and kicked up her board. "Seeing that we were heroes and saved Eva, do you think the Jade Emperor will let us go back to the Cloud Palace?"

"He did say if we did something good he would call us home," agreed Zu.

"Who knows?" said Monkey. "But I get the feeling our adventures are not over yet."

Bonus Bits!

Quiz Time

Can you answer these questions about the story? There are answers at the end (but no peeking before you finish!)

1. What do the men tell Sophie they need if she wants Eva back?

a)   1 million pounds

b)   2 million pounds

c)   5 million pounds

d)   10 million pounds

2. What were the leader's teeth like?

a)   dinosaur teeth

b)   knives

c)   tiger teeth

d)   snake fangs

3. What did Monkey's magic words make the skateboards do?

a)   travel faster along the road

b)   fly into the air

c)   spin sideways

d)   stop suddenly

4. What did Zu have to say to change his fork into a rake?

a)   upgrade

b)   full charge

c)   supersize

d)   super charge

5. Which of the characters knocked the leader down?

a)   Monkey

b)   Sandy

c)   Zu

d)   Eva

6. What did the black and white monkeys do when they saw Monkey?

a)   hid in their den

b)   screeched loudly

c)   jumped at the wire

d)   jumped up and down

7. What does Monkey ask Sophie B for?

a)   a selfie

b)   a mobile phone

c)   an autograph

d)   a reward

8. What did the men use to find Eva?

a)   spy pen

b)   helicopter

c)   GPS

d)   their eyes

9. What did the leader turn in to?

a)   a monkey king

b)   a snake demon

c)   a skeleton

d)   a serpent

10. What made the leader let go of Monkey?

a)   the police arrived

b)   Zu tripped him up

c)   his hands hurt when he touched Monkey

d)   the monkeys threw rocks at him

WHAT NEXT?

If you enjoyed reading this story and haven't already read *Skate Monkey: Demon Attack*, grab yourself a copy and curl up somewhere to read it! You'll enjoy finding out more about the characters from this book. Have a think about these questions after reading this story:

How do you think Eva felt when she was kidnapped?

- How do you think Sophie B felt when her daughter was kidnapped?
- Why do you think the men kidnapped Eva – what did they want?
- Do you think the Jade Emperor will let Monkey and his friends go back home now?

Why not write a letter in the role of Sophie B to the Jade Emperor to explain how helpful Monkey, Zu and Sandy have been. Can you try and convince him to take them back?

ANSWERS TO QUIZ TIME!

1B, 2D, 3B, 4C, 5A, 6D, 7A, 8C, 9B, 10D